THE WEDDING GIFT

Monica Withrington

PPR
PUBLISHING

For my friends Nick and Liz Hamlyn,
with thanks for their forbearance in
helping this little book and its many
companions towards publication.

Chapter I

Jupiter knows he had had enough warning.

"Not the daughter of Titus Marilius Gestus! Are you mad?" His cousin, Publius, had shaken his head in disbelief when Albanus had first voiced his intentions.

His colleagues at the Law Courts were almost as encouraging. "She's sixteen already. Practically a woman of the world. You'll have trouble with her, and no mistake!"

But it was his mother, Lucopania, who raised the most objection. And, unfortunately, her opinion counted the most of all.

"She's lived abroad. In Spain, no less, and North Africa. The gods only know what barbaric practices she may have picked up there!"

"It's you who's been nagging me to get married, Mother," Albanus had said wearily. "And what respectable family would be prepared to take me on, with my prospects?"

"Marriage was supposed to *improve* your prospects, not consign them to the sewers of Rome!" his mother had rasped. "You're a patrician, in case you've forgotten. You do not bear the name Albanus Cordelius Trivo for nothing. The family name of Cordelius still carries weight around here. Is *she* a patrician? No, I thought not. *Equites* – Middle-class: a merchant's daughter."

His mother spoke these last words as though she had just taken in a worm with her mouthful of lettuce and needed to extract it at once.

"Trajan, our beloved Emperor, has raised the status of the equestrian class, in case you'd forgotten," Albanus responded. "They're as respectable as the nobility, these days – and they have money."

"Money, is it? So that's what this is all about?" His mother drummed her fingers on the marble table top.

"You know I have debts, Mother, and not necessarily of my making. This house –"

"Ancestral home –"

"Costs a fortune to maintain. And poor Father left us with a creditor or three after paying my sisters' dowries."

"*They* made good marriages at least."

"And so shall I. The Gesti are honourable people."

"So, why aren't they better known? Who has ever heard of the Family Name of 'Marilius'? Besides, you ought to have a higher opinion of yourself. Lose a bit of weight and you'd be almost as handsome as your father."

"A pity I can't alter other things he passed on to me so easily, like growing back my missing hair, or reducing the size of my nose. Accept it, Mother. I'm a mediocre clerk, working for a mediocre lawyer. I'm thirty-seven years old, and, unfortunately, the last in the line of an old Roman family."

"And totally lacking in ambition," his mother cut in. "A Roman without ambition is no Roman at all –

just remember that!"

"I'm trying, Mother. For the family's sake, I shall make one more attempt to rise up the political ladder."

"And you think that an alliance with a family of the most dubious reputation will set you on that path, do you?"

"It's the best I can do."

"I'd call it a step into oblivion, myself, but there you are. Thank goodness your father is in the Land of the Blest, where he deserves to be – it would break his poor heart."

She lowered her head and, lifting the hem of her tunic, buried her face in it, making a series of snuffling noises that reminded Albanus of a foraging boar.

Here comes the emotional blackmail bit, he thought, a sense of despair crowding in on him. He might be of age in the eyes of the State, and therefore in a position to choose his own wife, but the State seemed to have overlooked the power of the Roman *matrona* in such matters. Without Lucopania's approval, marriage to Marilia Gesta, or any other girl, would be doomed before it had begun.

At last, she mopped her face and fixed her son with a glare.

"So, tell me. Where did you meet her, this girl you're so intent on marrying regardless of your poor mother's feelings?"

"I haven't, yet – met her I mean."

"This gets worse and worse! You're planning to

marry a girl you haven't even met? Can I remind you that Gaius Julius Caesar died one hundred and fifty years ago? With him, died the Republic. This is the Roman Empire, now. People don't go in for arranged marriages any more."

And more's the pity, thought Albanus. *That would solve all my problems in one.* He had never had the confidence of his friends, or even of his two sisters, Cordelia and Livilla. Making one's own social life – learning to charm the opposite sex, be at ease with them – had terrified the clumsy adolescent Albanus no less than it did the middle-aged, overweight one.

"I'm trying to tell you, Mother: nothing's settled. If we don't like each other, then the marriage quite simply won't happen."

"All right," said Lucopania, adjusting her commodious tunic about her ample person, "tell me this. How did you get mixed up with this family in the first place?"

Albanus sighed. "I did some business with her father – sought his advice while I was about it. He saw the dire state of our finances and said that the quickest way to get out of debt would be to marry a girl with a large dowry.

"In the next breath, he was telling me about his daughter. At first, I thought he was joking. But from the way he looked at me, I realised he wasn't. I asked to meet her, out of politeness more than any serious intention, but she happened to be out – sacrificing at the Temple of Diana. Her father says she's a very religious girl: never misses an opportunity to honour the gods."

Even this recommendation seemed to make little impression on Lucopania.

"Just 'happened to be out'," she sneered. "And what if you can't stand the sight of her – when she just happens to be in?"

She can have three heads with a wart on each of her three chins for all I care, thought Albanus, *just so long as marriage to her gets you and my creditors off my back.* Out loud, he said, "I'm sure she'll be perfectly presentable, Mother."

"And when do you hope to meet this paragon?"

"Tomorrow," Albanus said, the last iota of his fast fading enthusiasm suddenly evaporating.

Entering the home of the Gesti that first time had been rather daunting. It occupied a site on one of the spurs of the Esquiline Hill, with a splendid view of the Tiber. Everything, from the ornateness of the facade, to the excessive use of red and white marble, the garishness of the wall-paintings, obviously newly executed, to the unlimited number of slaves scurrying about, suggested recently acquired wealth. Freed slaves, perhaps...? Was he, Albanus, about to form an alliance with the lowest form of animal life still walking upright in Rome? He shuddered.

Now that he had time to think about it, Titus Gestus did have something of the foreigner about him: he might have shrewd, penetrating eyes, but he was also small and rabbity. And that accent... Albanus had first put it down to the number of years he had lived abroad, but now he wondered if he was, in fact, not a native Latin speaker at all. That he had picked the language up, piecemeal, in adult life. This pointed to one thing – captivity in a foreign land – and slavery.

Well, there was only one person on whom the blame rested: his mother. He and his two retainers, Galla and Bulba, might have grown old together quite pleasantly in their state of comfortable dilapidation, if she hadn't made it clear that she wanted her only son to follow the classic Roman path: a career in the army, followed by another in the law courts; and these leading to a toe-hold on the political ladder, with a strong woman behind him and, doubtless, a string of offspring to prove – Jupiter knows what? That he was a man?

Albanus's army career had ended almost before it had begun. His chronic chest complaint, which had plagued him from infancy, and prevented him from taking more than the lightest exercise in the gymnasium, had seen to that. Next, came the Law Courts. He was apprenticed to Quintus Govinius Mito, an advocate with the happy reputation for having lost more cases than anyone else in the past decade. Only the very poor and the hopeless sought his counsel. And remained poor and hopeless. Far from training the young would-be lawyer in the complexities of Roman Law, he had set Albanus to act as little more than his scribe. Albanus had tried to gain some knowledge for himself – he was not totally without initiative – and had appealed, once or twice, to other, more reputable, lawyers to take him on, but they had dismissed him, with a wave and a smile. The decay which was eating his master's brain was beginning to atrophy his, too. But, with little ambition, and the love of a peaceful and reclusive life, there seemed to Albanus to be no need to aspire to a successful career any more. Someone had to fill that space at the bottom of the heap, otherwise, surely, the more able would have nothing to trample on.

When, as he approached his thirty-fifth birthday, there appeared to be no wife on the horizon, however, Lucopania had taken the first steps to complicate his peaceful and uncomplicated life. True, the house hadn't seen a duster in many years, and was probably being held together more by the accumulation of dirt than by the crumbling mortar and sagging plasterwork, but did she have to take such extreme measures?

Trudging up the Caelian Hill from another dreary day of recording the long-winded speeches in the latest case his master was certain to lose, he had looked forward to nothing better than a long, cool cup of wine in the peristyle, as he gazed out at the little patch of meadow which had sprung up in place of what had once been a garden.

But, as he pushed open the front door to his abode, who should be filling in the *atrium* with her bulk but Lucopania. Flanked by two little girls. Little only in stature. One glance at their sullen faces, half turned away, one dark eye in each face scrutinising his shabby appearance with the sharpness of a small bird, and he was filled with a sense of deep foreboding. These were not girls, but young women, fully able to capture and compromise any unsuspecting male. But what was his mother doing in such company?

"Picked them up at the Market – for a song," Lucopania announced, cheerfully.

"Slaves?" Albanus exclaimed. "I've got Galla and Bulba to look after me. I don't need more slaves. I'll have to feed them for a start…"

"House slaves," Lucopania interrupted. "To clean your house. Keep it looking the way your father and I remember it."

Since the marriage of her elder daughter, Cordelia, to a wealthy farmer and heir to a large estate in the Sabine Hills, Lucopania, believing that her destiny had always been to live in a grander style by far than her marriage to Aulus had forced her to endure, had moved in with them.

"The house doesn't need a couple of girls to sweep and dust," Albanus had whimpered. "It needs a large legacy – to pay builders to stop it from falling down."

"The house needs a woman's hand. And two women are better than one. There are too many men in this establishment. Time you had a pretty face to look at."

Albanus sighed. His mother never acted out of one motive alone. There was always a scheme behind each action, which would come to light, usually, when he had dug himself in too deep to escape.

"But these are *slaves*," Albanus hissed at his

mother. "You're not expecting me to –"

"There are plenty of men – married ones, too – who find their female slaves rather – well, you know –" Lucopania raised one lavishly curved black brow.

Seeing his own mother behaving skittishly at her age completely unnerved him. He propped himself up against the wall.

"So, what are they called?" he asked.

"They're slaves. They don't have names."

"Then I shall give them names," Albanus said. Pointing a finger at the slightly taller, thinner one, he said, "I shall call you Maia. And you –" addressing the short squat one "– are Thalia. Can you speak Latin?"

"Of course they can speak Latin," snapped Lucopania. "They're Italian born – of foreign slave parents, no doubt, but they're fluent. I checked that before I bought them, naturally."

"And where am I to accommodate your new purchase, Mother?" Albanus asked. It wasn't as if she had bought him a couple of tunics and a toga, which he could store in a trunk. Slaves may not be thought by some of his fellow-citizens to be members of the human race, but they looked to Albanus to have all the usual attributes which defined that species. They would have to have some privacy, somewhere to sleep and somewhere to eat.

"There's space in the attic. Give them a couple of brushes and they can get rid of the mouse droppings. It will help them to get to know each other."

Six months later, Lucopania was disappointed to note that her latest attempts to interest her son in the female species had failed. He treated her purchases with the same deference as if they were a pair of goddesses. He left it to Galla to give them their orders, and if they chose not to obey, he kept a respectful distance. The dust continued to accumulate. The plaster continued to crumble. The wall paintings continued to fade, until they were little more than dirty smudges. Door curtains continued to hang as if by willpower alone. What the girls were actually getting up to was anyone's guess. They spent much of their time giggling in the attic bedroom which had been assigned to them. Of their master, they had no fear of sexual – or any other – advances.

So, when Lucopania seemed less than enthusiastic at the news that he had actually taken his first faltering steps on the road to matrimony, Albanus was left in a state of utter bewilderment.

"Do you want me to get married, or don't you?" he wailed in desperation.

"You know the answer to that one!" Lucopania snapped. "But not just to *anybody*. The gods know that you've taken long enough about it. I thought you were saving yourself for someone *special*."

Her rasping voice had taken on a pleading note. Albanus's heart sank. He disliked Lucopania most when she went all feminine on him and tried to appeal to his better nature. Why couldn't she just boss him around as usual? That was the mother he understood.

Chapter II

"Albanus, you look terrible! What's happened?" Marcus, his brother-in-law, and best friend from childhood, rose from his seat in Piso's Bar as Albanus staggered in. The bulging eyes and gaping mouth registered only one emotion: shock. Marcus helped him to a chair and signalled to the barman to bring a fresh jug of wine. "I thought you were going to meet the girl: is she...? Didn't you...?"

Albanus lifted the cup his friend had placed before him with a trembling hand and swallowed noisily.

"I met her," he said at last. "Oh, yes, I met her." He tossed the last of his wine down his throat and held the cup out for a refill.

"And...?"

"Oh, Marcus, what have I let myself in for?" Albanus ran his podgy fingers through what was left of his hair. "I thought –" he went on, "if she was a homely child – you know – plain, not very bright – I'd look after her: give her a happy life at least. The dowry her father's offering is – well - sort of vast: enough to pay off my debts and leave a bit over to have the house refurbished: that sort of thing – but – oh, the gods help me, not this!"

Marcus felt his own eyes growing wide.

"What is it, Albanus?" Was she missing some of her limbs, perhaps? Or maybe she had only one eye?

"You don't have to go through with this, you know. There are other women in Rome with large dowries. If she's so ugly that you can't bear to look at her –"

Albanus raised his head and stared in disbelief at his friend.

"Who says she's *ugly*? Did I say she was ugly? No – that's not the problem."

Marcus, now thoroughly baffled, mumbled, "So, what *is* the problem?"

"She's beautiful," Albanus half sobbed.

"She's – what did you say?"

"I said – she is beautiful." Albanus raised his voice, so that several heads turned in their direction. "Gorgeous – goddess-like – stunningly bea-u-ti-ful." These last words he spoke into the wine-cup, lovingly, as though it had just been transformed into his intended bride.

"You call that a problem?" Marcus queried.

"Wouldn't you? When she has all the unmarried men in Rome to choose from, why me?"

"You're.... not *that* bad."

"Fat, balding and in debt – that's what I am."

"So, you think there's a bit of coercion going on?"

"I've no idea what's going on. Her father introduced us and we drank a little wine – he keeps an excellent cellar, I'll grant him that. She and her mother sat side by side, holding hands."

"Nervous, was she?"

"Who – Marilia? Not a bit of it. It was her

mother she was consoling, not the other way round. Silvia Gesta looked terrified. No, Marilia took it all in her stride. When we had made small talk for about an hour, during which I'd played umpteen games of 'Five Stones' with her brother –"

"How did he get in on the act?"

"He's her *little* brother – about seven or eight – oh, Marcus do keep up! Well, her father asked her outright, in front of me, whether she would be willing to consider marrying me, and she fixed me with a look – oh, those eyes! So wide, so intense! As though she could see right inside me!"

"Go on," said his brother-in-law, now on the very edge of the bench.

"She nodded."

Marcus took a deep breath, leaned back, drained his cup and signalled to the barman for another jug.

"So – you're betrothed, then?"

"Not quite," said Albanus. "She said she'd consider it – that's all. But she's free to choose whom she likes – as you very well know. So, I ask you again – why didn't she turn me – me –" he patted the soft excesses of flesh on his stomach "– down flat?"

"Dubious family background, looking to better herself?" suggested Marcus. "She's not patrician, after all, and that still carries weight in these parts. If you suspect a hidden motive, then you'd better withdraw any offers for her hand now, before you get yourself into something you'll regret."

"That's not so simple any more," said Albanus,

raising the new jug and filling his cup to the brim. "You see – what I meant to happen was that this quiet, plain girl and I would, in time, feel a little tenderness towards each other, and grow old together in mutual harmony and companionship. But this girl has stolen my heart! In an instant, my life has been turned upside down. I'll be damned if I marry her, and damned if I don't."

The meeting had gone more or less as Albanus had described to his brother-in-law. From its perch overlooking the Tiber, the house provided a stunning view of the City, which spread out like a map below. The Tiber was a silver ribbon winding serenely between its banks where rows of neat little houses, their terracotta tiled roofs forming geometric patterns, were punctuated by the occasional tiny temple or patch of green.

On alighting from the litter that had carried him thus far, he had followed a short avenue of mature pine trees to where a secluded doorway, partially concealed by a flowering creeper, awaited him. The door itself was wide enough to let two carriages pass between the columns that flanked it, while the bronze knocker in the centre bore the face of a grinning satyr. Albanus had barely reached out his hand to lift it when the whole contraption swung inward, and he was invited into the dazzling gold and marble atrium by a small, eager janitor, whose grin echoed the door knocker itself.

There was barely time to take in the newly repainted and gilded entrance-hall, before Titus Marilius came hurtling towards him, taking him by the arm and leading him towards a portico from where the garden, with its abundance of trees and hedges, tumbled down the hillside towards a pond with a magnificent fountain.

Albanus was again struck, as on their first meeting, by Titus's shrewd, bright eyes, and felt, again, the stature of the man, which his height – the very lack of it – belied. And once again, his confidence returned that this man was sincere, and meant him only the best.

"Let me present my wife, Silvia," said Titus, leading him towards a delicate, pretty, young woman, her fair hair drawn up on to the top of her head, where it lay in tight curls, held in place by a series of shiny silver combs. No hint of grey, as yet. The eyes were bright, though a little tension played around the smile. A cool hand lay briefly in Albanus's, and a soft voice sounded some sort of greeting. Suddenly, it was brought home to him the enormity of what he was taking on. Silvia was expected to give up her only daughter to this clumsy stranger – and what a disappointment that must be!

Despite his morning at the Baths, Albanus felt shabby in his ancient tunic and threadbare toga, a poor offering for a family which made up in charm and style what they lacked in status. It also struck him that such a couple – for he now saw that Titus, too, was good-looking in a diminutive, dark and foreign way – might just not have a cross-eyed, three-legged daughter.

And at that moment, two people burst into the portico. A small boy of about eight, holding high a small bronze ornament, was followed by a girl, not much taller, her pale pink tunic floating out behind her as she ran. Silvia put out an arm and restrained the boy, who protested and struggled, while the girl slid to a halt on seeing that the household had a visitor. Two huge eyes in a heart-shaped face fixed their gaze on him. Her cheeks, already flushed from running, now glowed even more, as she realised just who this stranger might be.

The children were ordered to sit, which they did, either side of their mother. Every now and again, the one reached behind their parent, in an attempt at pushing the other off the seat, while trying, without success, not to break into silent giggles. Meanwhile, introductions were made and wine was passed round.

Albanus's first urge was to make a run for it and escape, now, before he was trapped for ever. But he knew that his legs would not let him. He was glued to the marble seat he had been invited to occupy, and all his bones had turned to jelly. How soon he would be able to take his leave without causing offence, he did not know, but he had never felt so out of place.

However, as he had described to Marcus, the one person who seemed completely at ease was Marilia herself. Her smile contained real warmth. She answered his polite inquiries as to her health and general wellbeing with composure, and even some humour. Sextus, her little brother, kept turning to his mother and whispering questions, while keeping one eye fixed on Albanus's face. Like his sister, he, too, had inherited their father's sharp gaze. Albanus felt himself in a room full of scrutinizing eyes. *How to get out of here with his dignity intact?* he kept asking himself.

But Titus was in no hurry to let him go. He clearly wanted his daughter to gain as much of an impression of him as she could in the shortest possible time. So, aided by the best quality wine he had ever tasted, Albanus allowed himself to relax. Whatever the outcome, he reasoned, he could at least enjoy the moment.

"Delicious wine," he heard himself murmur. It was not too sweet, but with an aroma he couldn't quite define. At once, the slave nearest his elbow refilled his goblet.

Albanus winked at Sextus, who immediately ducked shyly under his mother's arm, then bobbed up and asked, "Do you play Five Stones?"

"Sextus –" Marilia scolded, and her mother added, "The gentleman hasn't come to play with you –"

But this was precisely what Albanus needed. "I haven't had the chance to play it for a long time," he said, "but I used to be rather good at it. Shall we have a game?"

Excitedly, the little boy rushed back into the house and returned a few minutes later with a board and coloured stones. Pulling up a small, folding table and a chair, the child plonked himself in front of his prospective brother-in-law and proceeded to lay out the stones.

Soon the two of them were absorbed in their game. Albanus sensed the family's approval wrap itself around him. *How I would love to be a part of this family*, he thought, with sudden warmth. *If only...* But Marilia was too good a catch for him. This was all going to end in tears. Especially when, to his surprise and embarrassment, her father inquired of Marilia what she thought of him as a possible husband.

When, at last, Albanus had felt he had stood the scrutiny of the women long enough, and was taking his leave, Titus followed him through the heavy, carved front door.

"So," said the merchant, "what do you think?"

"Of Marilia? Why, she's charming – a delightful girl." Albanus meant every word.

"And? Do you think you could marry her, given time?"

"I'm sure I'd be delighted – if such a girl agreed to marry me."

"Then we might as well go ahead –"

"Shouldn't we give your daughter time to reconsider –" What if she was merely being polite. "I want her to like me at least."

"She'll like you all right," said Titus. "Have no fear of that."

"But – I don't want to spoil her life by forcing her in any way. She must come willingly or not at all."

"I understand. But as for spoiling her life, as you put it –- believe me, if anyone's life gets spoiled, it won't be hers."

The afternoon was well advanced by the time Albanus

parted from Marcus and struggled up the Caelian Hill to his own shabby house. He should not have been sweating quite so much, he thought, with the sun beginning its descent, and a cool breeze coasting towards him from the summit. And did the trees have to sway quite so dizzily? The first time he reached for the knocker he missed, jarring his fingers on the solid wooden door instead.

"Oh, Hades!" he swore, slurring the last 's'. At the second try, his hand made contact with the brass ring, just as he felt his knees give way under him. He sagged on to the dusty cobbles, still clasping the knob. Suddenly, he was being dragged forwards, until, letting go, he seemed to be tumbling right into the dribbling jaws of an enormous dog. But, instead of the beast devouring him, his bulk smacked on to the cold floor of the lobby where he lay, staring into one bloodshot eye, which, like the rest of the animal, formed part of the mosaic floor decoration. Below the spread front paws, gold lettering picked out the warning: *CAVE CANEM* (Beware of the Dog).

A hand reached down and drew him gently to his feet. Albanus opened his eyes and tried to bring the two overlapping faces of his faithful janitor, Galla, into focus.

"I expect you would like a little nap, Master," said the elderly slave, calmly and without emotion, as he led his master slowly across the atrium towards a faded curtain concealing a doorway.

"Just let me die," Albanus begged. "Oh, gods,

why did I have to be born a Roman? Tell me that, Galla. Why?"

Albanus floated on a giant water-lily pad to a distant island peopled by swans. Suddenly, a gust of wind caught the sails of his craft, which was swept on to the shore at speed, spilling its cargo head-first on to the rocks.

"Ouch!" cried Albanus.

"Son! Not that you're worthy of that name these days." What was his mother doing on an island of swans, birds sacred to Venus?

"Get up! You look so undignified lying half out of bed, with your head on the floor. Don't tell me you've been drinking again."

Albanus tried to swivel his head, but his neck seemed locked, somehow. The only solution was to allow the rest of his body to follow his upper half, and right himself, once all of him was on the same level. When he did finally manage to bring himself into a sitting position, leaning against the sleeping-couch, it was no thanks to the bed sheet, which had wound itself around him like a shroud.

"Water! Bring me water!" His tongue felt like the arena in the Colosseum.

"So, this is how you celebrate your betrothal?" his mother was saying, although her voice seemed to be in two keys at once. "And just when I've decided to give you my blessing."

"So-sorry – I didn't hear that," spluttered

Albanus thickly. "I thought I heard you say something about a blessing."

"On your *marriage*, yes," his mother was saying. "I've brought you a little present – a wedding gift."

Albanus opened one eye. He peered at his mother. There seemed to be even more of her than usual. He closed that eye and tried with the other. Yes, there was rather a lot of her. She seemed to have four arms, two heads and an unknown number of feet.

"Look, Albanus. What do you think? This is Metaxus. He's a Greek. Newly arrived on a slave-ship at Ostia, yesterday. Doesn't speak much Latin, yet, but *you've* had a good education. Now's your chance to practice the Greek you learned at school."

"Mother!" Which of them was the more drunk? wondered Albanus. "I'm getting married – *if* I get married – to a Roman girl. I don't need a slave to practice Greek on."

"But you do need a gardener!" exclaimed his mother. "You won't win Fair Lady when she's standing knee-high in nettles. So, I've brought you Metaxus. He's young and strong. And I've no doubt weeds grow just the same where he comes from."

"Just send for Galla, will you, Mother? Get him to deal with this."

Between them, Galla and Bulba, the cook, managed to concoct something which fizzed and hissed in the cup as though it was trying to escape, and which, once administered, miraculously restored their master to the point where he was no longer seeing double. Now that he was able to look properly at his wedding gift, he had to admit that his mother had found a rarity. Lithe and delicately made, his lightly muscled body a honey colour turning to bronze, the young Greek would have looked perfectly at home on a plinth outside a temple or a public building.

"You born – how many years?" Albanus asked, wrenching his schoolboy Greek from its moorings deep within the furthest cavern of his mind.

Metaxus raised his fingers – all ten – once, then those of his right hand and the thumb and forefinger of his left.

"Seventeen? Good."

"You do – garden?" He made a shovelling gesture, at which the young slave grinned, not even trying to conceal his amusement. Didn't this arrogant youth realise that a slave could be sentenced to death for making fun of his master?

"Galla!" he bellowed. "Show this brat where we keep our gardening things. Set him to work."

"Pardon, Master, we have no gardening implements."

"Then, here –" he threw his leather pouch at the janitor, who had to take a hasty step backwards to avoid being winded by it "– take him to the market and buy some – get whatever he needs."

"But, Master, I never learned Greek."

"Then shout," said Albanus. "He'll get the message soon enough."

Chapter III

Albanus was seated at the tiny desk in his study, trying to will the figures on a tablet to reverse themselves: the debits to cross over to the credit side and the credits to the debit. But they absolutely refused to obey him, as did the vision of a pair of enormous blue eyes in a small, heart-shaped face, that refused to disappear from his tortured mind. Marcus had been right, of course. So had his cousin Publius and his friends at the law-courts: the daughter of Titus Marilius Gestus would only bring him anguish and heartache. But how to eradicate her from his thoughts? She had come to haunt his every waking hour, not to mention his dreams as well. And time – all of the thirty-six hours since they had first met – had done nothing to alleviate his longing, but rather had intensified it.

There was a shuffling in the doorway and the sound of someone clearing his throat.

"Yes, Galla, what is it?" Albanus asked, without looking up.

"Pardon me, Master," the old slave wheezed. "You have visitors."

"Visitors? How many visitors?"

"The Lady Cordelia, Master, and Master Horreus, Master." Did a cloud just pass over the garden? Albanus wondered. What on earth could have brought his elder sister down from her mountain habitat? He rolled up the ledger and pushed it roughly into the box by his side, so that the edges creased and tore slightly. Then he rose and stomped past the janitor and out into the atrium.

Cordelia Lucopanilla filled the space between two of the supporting pillars in the atrium with as much ease as her mother. Indeed, looking at his sister was like seeing his mother, only twenty years younger. The same broad forehead, wide-set eyes, disappearing into their copious pouches, bulbous nose and flabby lips, painted the brightest ruby. Chin and neck were ill-defined, owing to the sac of skin which linked them. Across the well-padded shoulders and rounded arms, a generously proportioned tunic strained. In short, Cordelia was a big girl. She was ten years younger than Albanus, and already the mother of five – three sons and two daughters.

The last time she and Albanus had met had been for the funeral of their father, Aulus. It had been about a year after the arrival of her third child and second son, if his memory served him rightly. She never visited the family house in Rome, except for the most exceptional reason, and he had never been invited to the farm in the Sabine Hills. And, yet, here she was, in all her statuesque grandeur, her marsh reed of a husband cowering behind her.

"Mother –" Albanus began "– Is Mother all right?" Had she fallen ill? Died? What else could have brought both of them here – and with not one of their growing brood in tow?

"Who? Mother? Nooo – she's in fine spirit," came the reply. She had even developed the same rasp as their mother, Albanus noticed. He had always believed that it had been a mistake letting the two of them spend so many of their days together. How had Horreus stood it for all these years?

So – could this be a social visit, after all? He turned to Galla, who was hovering in the shadows, as if he suspected that Albanus might need a bodyguard – though what good he might be as either a physical or moral support was questionable.

"Wine, please Galla?" Then he whispered, "The brown jar – the one nearest the door – on the right." Albanus saw no reason for bringing out his best wine even if this was a rather unusual occasion.

"No need to waste the day in the shadows," he said cheerfully to his visitors. "Let's drink what Galla brings us in the peristyle." At least, thanks to his mother's premature wedding gift, the garden was almost tamed. "I expect Mother told you about the new gardener?"

"She's talked about little else," Horreus dared to say.

"That and the wedding itself – all settled, is it?" asked Cordelia, sweeping through the study, whose doors led into the garden.

"Hardly," her brother replied. "We've met once, that's all. I can't understand the fuss all this seems to be causing."

"And? Do you think you might go ahead?"

The eyes gleamed in their pouches.

"How do I know? It's up to them – all of them — the mother included."

"So you're still happy about bringing disgrace on our heads by marrying into a family with no background – freedmen for all we know?"

"Not that again. Mother didn't send you, did she, to try talking me out of this?"

As Galla shuffled out into the peristyle with a tray of cups spilling wine, he seized one roughly before even offering any to his guests.

"Not at all," Cordelia snorted. "Quite the opposite. She's full of it: thinks you've made a brilliant match – you'd think she was talking about your finding a wife among the daughters of the Emperor himself. Went on about it so much that even Horreus felt it was time we saw the situation for ourselves – didn't you, dear?"

The little man nodded his head vigorously.

"Well, you see the situation as you find it — nothing has changed. The wedding won't be going ahead."

"*Really?* Mother was so certain –"

"That was before I actually met Marilia."

"That bad, was she? Oh, good. I'm so relieved. I hope you realise the bother you've caused – Horreus and I having to desert the children like this to come all the way down here to Rome – but, at least, we shan't have to come again."

"No." Albanus agreed flatly. "You won't have

to come here again. Were you hoping to stay to dinner, by the way? Only I'll have to instruct Bulba if you are –"

"Oh, no, no, no," said Cordelia, wrinkling up her blunt bell-push of a nose. "Bulba's cooking can only have got worse in all these years, and I can still remember the last meal I ate here. Repeated on me all night. No, we've got an invitation from Fulvia, Horreus's sister, and Garrulus, her husband, thank you. Thought we ought to call in on Livilla and Marcus and the girls, while we're in the neighbourhood, as well."

Cordelia tossed the last of the wine into her cavernous mouth, winced at the sharpness and heaved herself upright. She and Horreus took their leave without much ceremony. There was no sense of loss on either side. Albanus accompanied them to the front door and politely handed his sister into the waiting litter, noting that her husband had chosen not to ride with her. It was going to be hard enough on the bearers without Horreus's additional weight, however insignificant.

He watched the bearers struggling down the street with their burden until they disappeared below the brow of the hill, then returned to his study with a sigh. He had just taken the ledger out of its case once more, and was trying to straighten its crumpled edge when the shuffling sound so familiar to his ears made him turn towards the doorway for the second time in an hour.

"A gentleman and his good wife, and their young son and daughter, Master," Galla bleated.

Albanus leaped to his feet; his chair went flying

and the ledger slithered on to the floor.

"Name? What name did they give?"

The startled slave gulped as he backed away from his advancing master.

"Er – Gestus – Marilius Gestus."

They were ranged in a semi-circle around the impuvium. Smiling warmly, Titus took a step forward at Albanus's arrival.

"Hope we've caught you at a good time, my friend," he said, reaching out both his arms. "We thought, as we were passing –"

"Of course, of course!" Albanus suddenly felt the air about him grow lighter. What a genial atmosphere surrounded this strange little man and his family! Away from them, he was plunged into the deepest gloom, besieged by apprehension and doubt. But let them once appear, and he felt like dancing. He gave Silvia the customary greeting and moved on to Sextus, their young son, who raised a clenched fist, to which Albanus added his knuckles in a playful punch.

Finally, he allowed his eyes to rest on the sweet face of Marilia. She fixed him with that steady gaze he remembered at their first meeting, and he felt his head spin. Holding both her tiny hands in his, he spoke to the whole party.

"Let us take a cup of wine in the peristyle," he said. "Galla!" he called to his retainer. "Some wine, please – the jar at the back of the cellar."

"But, Master," Galla began, "your mother – the

Lady Lucopania – said that had to be kept –"

"*Now*, Galla! I want it now!"

As he led the party towards the cool colonnade enclosing his modest garden, he noticed that Marilia was taking in all she saw of the house – the peeling plaster, the faded wall paintings and those ragged apologies for door curtains. But, when they emerged into the sunshine, she exclaimed, "Now that's a fine sight!"

Albanus's smile faded as quickly as it had formed. Where on earth had Metaxus materialised from? Here he was, darting from flowerbed to flowerbed, snipping, trimming, pulling up unwanted greenery: anyone might have mistaken him for the god Mercury, descended from on high for a spot of weeding. Was Marilia admiring his handiwork, or the gardener himself? Both Albanus's elation and his heart nose-dived towards his leather sandals.

"Metaxus – shoo!" he ordered the slave, but Marilia and her mother raised a protest.

"Let him stay," Silvia said, a glint in her eye.

And her daughter added demurely, "He's not in our way."

"We're actually here to ask you to dinner the day after tomorrow," Titus said, seating himself beside his wife on the stone bench in the cool shade of the peristyle. "Marilia would like to get to know more about you, wouldn't you, my dear?"

The girl smiled charmingly, and the arc of fair curls around her face bobbed in agreement.

The conversation progressed pleasantly in the

warm afternoon, everyone relaxing more with each refill from the venerable wine jar.

What would Cordelia have to say, now? Albanus wondered. And by what favourable twist of Fate had his sister and the Gesti family missed each other? They must have passed on the road, but Cordelia and Horreus would have had no idea that this little foursome were headed towards the very door by which they had just left the old family home.

Albanus searched his mind for something agreeable to say to his potential wife.

Sorry about the state of the house — needs a woman's hand, you know, fortunately stuck in his throat. It was too banal for words.

But the Gesti had their own way of putting him at his ease. "This garden boy —" Titus said, "— not a bad specimen."

"Just a little something my mother picked up at the market," Albanus joked. "A gift for me, she said. She's inclined to make these impulsive buys from time to time, I'm afraid." They didn't need to know his mother's real motive in buying the slave.

"I wish my impulsive buys showed such good judgement," Marilia remarked. "Do you think she could teach me?"

"Now, you won't —" Albanus stopped himself just in time from saying *You won't want to meet my mother — she gives horses a fright —* and finished with "— want to let my mother lead you astray."

"Yes I would — well, not astray, exactly. I have

every confidence she could be a good influence on me.”

“Does she live nearby?” Silvia asked.

“Er, no. Sabine Hills – with my sister. Finds the air more to her liking.”

“I don’t blame her for that,” put in Marilia. “I find Rome disgustingly stuffy. Do you go to your sister’s often?”

At that moment, the wine jug dried up and Albanus called for another of his mother’s ‘specials’.

“You do keep a good cellar,” Titus remarked. *Once again, my mother’s doing*, thought Albanus.

“Thank you, sir,” he said instead. How kind of these people to keep off the subject of the house, and his all-too obvious poverty. But there was something in the name ‘Cordelius’, he supposed. A tingle of misapprehension rippled between his shoulder-blades. He couldn’t put off the nasty thought any longer. They were after one thing: high birth, just as he was after a few thousand sesterces. They were willing to give away their daughter, just as in the days of the Republic, for a position in Roman society. But he needed their money more. Could he honestly bring himself to dirty his hands in this way – ruining the life of a young girl into the bargain?

Little Sextus, soon bored with the grown-ups’ talk, leaped from his seat and charged at Metaxus, whooping like an Etruscan bandit. The pair spent what was left of the visit chasing and teasing each other, finally engaging in a game of shadow-fighting – all much to the amusement of the onlookers. As the fierceness went out of the sun, so Albanus relaxed, soaking up the company who had chosen to pass the afternoon in his garden.

"So, you will come to our little dinner party, then?" Silvia asked, as the family took their leave.

"Come a little early," Titus said softly in Albanus's ear. "We can discuss the – you know what." He tapped his nose.

Chapter IV

The Gesti certainly knew how to throw a party. Slaves scurried back and forth, carrying garlands, torches, table decorations and all the other paraphernalia which seemed necessary for what Titus had termed a 'modest family celebration'. Sextus was behaving like a puppy, scampering in and out of the legs of the adults, joyfully tripping up slaves and freeborn alike

Albanus reeled out of Titus's study some time later, believing that death had just bypassed him altogether and he had gone straight to Elysium. Titus had been more than generous with regard to the proposed dowry. However, there would be a price to pay: he was thinking of marrying a girl who would keep him on his toes, so Titus had warned him. Indolence was not a word in Marilia's vocabulary, apparently.

Still thinking himself in the Land of the Blest, Albanus found a beautiful nymph awaiting him in the atrium. Her long, white tunic was shot through with silver and she had the face of Marilia.

"Mama says I should walk with you in the garden, until the other guests arrive," she said, in Marilia's silken voice.

The Gesti's garden was, unlike his own, which filled a central courtyard, enclosed by the house on only three sides. Otherwise, it had burst forth from the confines of the peristyle to spill down a series of broad terraces, flanked by flowerbeds, and hedges concealing their own secrets.

But it was beside the splendid, three-tiered fountain, its carved fauns cavorting with the naiads – the garden's focal point – that the pair eventually stopped.

"Are you happy?" Albanus asked, as they stood, mesmerised by the water which leaped and danced.

Marilia gazed up at him, her eyes wide and full of innocence. "Of course I'm happy," she replied. "Why shouldn't I be?"

Albanus hesitated. "I just wondered – there are so many younger, handsomer men in Rome –"

"And each one a Narcissus – in love with his own looks," Marilia interrupted. "Besides, younger men go to war. I'd hardly see him – whoever he was."

"You'll find my home very different from your parents'."

Marilia smiled her most charming smile, which sent Albanus's head into a spin.

"At least it won't be boring in your house, Albanus. On the contrary, there'll be any amount of things for me to do."

And she rose up on tiptoe and planted a kiss on Albanus's sagging jowl before declaring, "Oh, look, I do believe our first guests have arrived."

As she started to run towards the house, the moon, newly risen, picked out the silver threads in her tunic. Diana, moon goddess and protectress of all young, unmarried creatures, was shining favourably on her handmaid, it seemed.

Albanus stood still for a moment, fingering his lower jaw. What were those last words? Something about finding plenty to do in his house? His mind raced from the house's general condition, in sorry need of a woman's hand, to the memory of Metaxus flexing his muscles in the garden. *Oh, Marilia*, he murmured. *You of the guileless, steady gaze, yet giving so little away: Enigma should be your name.*

But, with that chaste kiss, Albanus knew that his fate, whatever it might be, was sealed.

CAVE CANEM

Chapter V

Any further doubts that Albanus might have had about his mother's blessing on his marriage to Marilia Gesta were finally dispelled when she oversaw the cleaning of his toga herself. She took it to the fuller, who laundered it and returned it a gleaming white that almost blinded its owner. She also presented him with a new tunic, having torn the old one into dusters so that the two lazy slave girls, Maia and Thalia, might justify their bed and board for a change.

One flaming hot day in June, the month sacred to Juno, goddess of marriage, Albanus and Marcus met at the public baths and spent several hours being steamed, oiled, scraped and perfumed, emerging at last like a pair of young gods about to ascend to the foot of the throne of Jupiter.

Since the betrothal, Titus Marilius Gestus and his sweet wife, Silvia, had shown Albanus the extent of their hospitality. There had been a formal invitation to another dinner party, in honour of the young couple, and less formal occasions when he had dined with them anyway. He liked them more and more. Titus seemed less rabbity, more relaxed, now that his daughter's future had been secured. Once, Albanus and Marilia had managed a stroll in the moonlit garden, and he had placed a tentative kiss on her cheek. Her response had almost landed them both in the fishpond. She had flung

37

a pair of slender arms about his neck. Unprepared, he had staggered backwards and would have slid, with her, into the chilly depths had she not grabbed hold of his tunic and pulled him the other way. They fell in a heap on the soft, dry turf. There seemed little point in rising at once. Time had passed so pleasantly, in fact, that only when they heard Marilia's personal maid, Rebekah, calling did they realise that dusk had long given way to night.

Thus it was that Albanus stepped out on his wedding-day, considerably more self-assured than he had on the day of his betrothal. A litter conveyed him and Marcus up the Esquiline Hill to the grand abode of the Gesti. In the fierce heat of mid-afternoon, he was thankful that he could be carried in comfort.

Inside the atrium, which was so bedecked by garlands and baskets of flowers swinging from every archway, that it could have been mistaken for a hanging garden, the pair were surrounded by a cheerful throng. Albanus greeted his younger sister, Livilla, her husband, Marcus, and their three little daughters, before going on to welcome his cousin, Publius. Albanus was relieved to see that even he had not deserted him, despite his earlier expressions of doubt at the prospect of the marriage.

Publius's wife, Pomponia, stood by his side, tall and elegant, while, flanking them were their impeccable twin sons, Crispinus and Lucanus. In their identical, snow-white tunics under their boyhood purple-bordered togas, they closely resembled marble statues, and seemed almost as alive.

Little Sextus, too, was swathed in a toga so large, that it trailed behind him like some sort of incongruous bed-sheet. Since he was unable to stand still for more than half a minute at a time, the garment was continually unwinding itself, keeping his personal tutor, an elderly Egyptian, fully and rather pointlessly employed in retrieving it.

Suddenly, from a side room, Marilia and her bridesmaid, a portly matron of about thirty-five, appeared. The bride wore the customary yellow shawl, draped over her white linen tunic, which was without a hem. A flaming red and orange veil covered the upper part of her face. In a dream, Albanus approached, reached out a hand and clasped her tiny fingers. He gave them a gentle squeeze and thrilled to feel their pressure returned.

Giving the couple a nod, Titus led them to the family altar in the atrium, to begin the sacrifice. A spidery little man hovered by his side. This creature was the *auspex*, whose vital task it was to read the entrails of the calf, once slain, and appease the gods by pronouncing a good or bad future for the couple.

Alblanus was too squeamish – or was that cowardly? – to witness the calf's final moments, and squeezed his eyes shut as the priest raised the sword above the young creature, lying tethered on the altar.

Following its slaughter, its stomach was opened with one slash to reveal its entrails. They lay on the right side of the carcass – pronounced a good omen by the auspex.

Relieved, Albanus offered his bride a ring of gold, speaking the words which expressed the spiritual equality between the wedded couple within the marriage: *"Ubi tu Gaia, ego Gaius"* (when you are Gaia, I shall be Gaius), to which Marilia responded shyly, *"Ubi tu Gaius, ego Gaia."*

Incense filled the turgid air while prayers to Jupiter, King of the gods, were said. Then the whole company began a joyful hymn to the god of marriage, as they followed the newly-weds through the house and into the brilliant, sun-lit garden.

As Albanus and his bride, her veil now lying carelessly about her shoulders, accepted the greetings of their guests, they introduced them to one another. Lucopania was excelling herself, by causing as much offence as possible. While praising the Gesti's house and everything in it, she managed to squeeze in some pointed remarks about the Cordelian clan representing 'old' money.

"No money, don't you mean?" muttered Albanus under his breath.

"There's been a Cordelian living on the Caelian Hill since the foundation of the City," she announced to all present.

"I wouldn't say that too loudly, Mother, if I were you," Livilla laughed. "Romulus, our Founder, filled his new City with riff-raff, or so the historians tell us – murderers and common criminals on the run. That's hardly anything to boast about!"

Marilia rolled her eyes and, grinning, turned towards her husband, shaking her head in disbelief.

"Sorry," Albanus whispered back. "It's the only mother I've got."

His colleagues from the Law Courts had turned out, presumably to gloat and say, "I told you so," but all seemed overwhelmed by Marilia's charm and beauty. On Marilia's side, there were neighbours and business acquaintances, but not a whiff of a relative. Albanus presumed them all to be still in Spain.

Central to the feast would be the calf, now turning on its spit, while wine flowed and the guests partook of other appetising morsels, olives, nuts and stuffed dormice. Couches had been arranged on the terrace, on which the men reclined, and the women sat. Some deity had apparently breathed life into the impeccable sons of Publius, who, having discarded their togas, were now noisily chasing each other around the fountain. Albanus suspected that deity to be Dionysus, since he had noticed earlier how the boys had shunned their own goblets of well-watered wine in favour of their parents' stronger mixture, when Publius and Pomponia were not looking. Suddenly there came a cry and a loud splash, as Crispinus – or was it Lucanus? – could be seen flailing his arms among the reeds and the water-lilies in the fishpond. His brother, Lucanus – or was it Crispinus? – in trying to rescue his brother, overbalanced and joined him, much to the alarm, no doubt, of the carp resident there.

Pomponia, losing her dignity and composure in

one, began screaming loudly enough to rouse Pluto on his kingly throne in the Land of the Dead, while the men in the party hurried across the lawn, preparing to risk soaking their togas in the muddy depths to save her sons. But before any of them were within a javelin's length of the pond, the twins were seen lying on the grass, retching and sobbing. Sextus, it seemed, had pulled them out single-handed, and was now standing over them, feet apart like a miniature Caesar surveying his conquests, his hands resting on his bony hips.

"What's the fuss all about?" Marilia muttered to her husband. "It's only water."

"It's not that," Albanus explained with a grin. "They're supposed to be impeccable. Falling into fishponds is not what they do."

Marilia's shoulders began to shake. Albanus reached out a hand in alarm. But, as the tears spilled down her cheeks, he realised that she was laughing.

"Your family!" she spluttered. "You're all half mad." Then, as she wiped her eyes, she added, "Any more oddballs I should know about?"

Albanus thought for a moment. "Well, there's Cordelia," he said. "My older sister."

"She's not here?"

"Luckily, she couldn't make it – expecting her sixth, I believe – or is it her seventh? I lose count. But, if you can imagine my mother, twenty years younger – give or take – then that's Cordelia!"

Silvia had the now not-so-Impeccable Ones transported into the house, where they could be divested of their sodden tunics. She had already worked out that their vomiting on the grass had been only partly due to their having ingested any pond water. Either way, they were both an ugly shade of green. Since they were needed for the all-important 'Fetching Home' Ceremony at the end of the feast, she deemed it a good idea if they were put to bed for a few hours.

As dusk descended on the City, the Fetching Home began. Albanus had first to wrest his bride from the arms of her mother. Marilia made the most of this part of the ceremony, shrieking and giggling as she was borne away. Silvia looked less happy, but was soon comforted by a horde of female guests.

Next, the whole party gathered outside the house and set off in procession down the Esquiline to Albanus's home. Sextus, his toga firmly pinned up out of the way of his feet with one of Silvia's dress pins, stepped out in the lead, his bony knees buckling as he struggled with an enormous burning torch. The gleaming white of the twins' togas served to intensify the grey-green of their young faces, as each took a hand of the bride and attempted to lead her to her new home. Walking proved to be a problem, however, so that it was Marilia who did the leading. At intervals, as the trio wove about the street, she was obliged to pull one or other of them upright, before he sagged on to the cobbles.

The other guests followed behind, singing with greater exuberance than before, though keeping in time less, and banging cymbals with no co-ordination whatsoever. Outside Albanus's house on the Caelian Hill, the happy party halted. Marilia anointed the doorposts with oil which she covered with wool, then waited for the twins to carry her over the threshold of her new home. But they were no more capable of lifting a girl even as small and dainty as Marilia, than flying to the moon.

There was only one solution: Marilia whirled round and launched herself into her husband's unsuspecting arms. This action dislodged Albanus's toga, and he tripped over the wretched garment, stumbling towards his open front door. As the porch floor, with its mosaic of the snarling dog and the warning *CAVE CANEM,* came hurtling towards him for a second time, Galla, waiting inside, snatched the bride to safety.

Albanus found himself eyeball to bloodshot eyeball with the beast once more. "We meet again," he mumbled into its dribbling jaws. But another thought was swirling round inside his head – far more alarming. Only one of the words above the animal's head was visible from that angle: *CAVE!* (Beware!)

"Not a good omen," thought Albanus. "Definitely *not* a good omen."

Chapter VI

Now came the moment which Albanus had both longed for and dreaded: the preparation of the bride in her chamber, and his part in making the marriage complete. He wondered whether he should use the Emperor Augustus's example and lead a platonic life with Marilia. Perhaps she would be more comfortable with that. She was so beautiful: who was he to violate that beauty?

But, as he approached the bridal chamber, he knew that that could never be. Wearing a newly-laundered tunic, which Galla had insisted he change into, his hair – what was left of it – carefully combed down to his ears and reeking of some exotic perfume, he accepted his fate.

Rebekah drew back the door curtain to reveal his bride, draped in the finest silk, her hair in a loose cascade on to the bank of pillows against which she now reclined. Her blue eyes danced when she saw her new husband, and she reached out her slender arms, drawing him on to the bridal bed with surprising strength. Albanus was barely aware of the door curtain being discreetly drawn across their privacy.

"By Hercules!" she greeted her husband. "What's that smell? You reek like an Egyptian market!"

"Galla's idea," Albanus apologised. "He thought you might need a little help? Like an aphrodisiac?" The last word came out as little more than a whisper.

"Me? Need an aphrodisiac?" Marilia let out an unladylike guffaw. "Come here, Husband. I'll show you what I need. Last night I left all my toys on the altar of Diana, in the fashion of all Greek and Roman girls, on the eve of their entering womanhood," Marilia whispered. "I want to belong to Juno, now, the guardian of marriage. It is for you to make it so."

Then, before he could make any appropriate moves himself, she launched herself at him, with all the modesty of a bolt leaving its ballista, while playfully lifting his tunic over his head and hurling it into the furthest corner of the room. There was no possibility of resistance, now. The girl's determination saw to that. Had she done this before? Albanus didn't care. She wanted him, and that was all that mattered.

And, as they were finally joined in marital bliss, did she squeal with pleasure or pain? Her squeals were mingled with shouts of laughter, and Albanus could only imagine the startled expressions on the faces of the slaves keeping guard on the other side of the curtain.

Later, as she rested her head on his chest, she emitted a happy sigh.

"Tomorrow I shall make a sacrifice to Juno," she murmured before slipping into a contented sleep.

Too soon, however, the half-bad omen began to kick in – during their first evening meal alone, in fact.

"By the Divine Emperor Claudius!" exclaimed Marilia, grimacing. "This food is disgusting! What is it? Putrefying cat?"

"It's Bulba's speciality," said Albanus, blushing for his ageing cook. "Boiled rabbit in fish sauce."

"Well, this rabbit must have died a long time ago – of old age. We need a new cook."

"But Bulba's been in the family since he was a boy."

"Then he's earned his freedom ten times over. Besides –" she reached over and patted her husband's well-rounded girth with her small hand, "– his cooking is doing nothing for your waistline."

"Yes, but –" As Marilia continued to fix him with her wide-eyed, expectant gaze, he cleared his throat. "The truth is – we shouldn't be spending money on a new cook, not just yet." *Not until the debts are paid off and we know what we have left after the house has had its renovations done,* he thought.

"That's because you indulge in luxuries like gardeners, when what you need is a decent cook!"

"The boy, Metaxus, was my mother's idea – a wedding gift, remember."

Marilia stared down at her plate, and a large tear, rolling down her cheek, plopped on to the grey mess congcaling there.

"I thought –" she began, "I *thought* I had married a man with a future. Instead, I seem to have lumbered myself with a third-rate lawyer's clerk whose mother buys his slaves for him."

Albanus felt his face grow hot. "I'm doing my best," he said. "I'll be a lawyer soon – it's just that the openings –"

"– snap shut the moment you put in an appearance." Then, seizing his wrist in a surprisingly strong grip, she began to speak urgently. "I want to be proud of you, my husband. I want to see you rise up the political ladder. Why, at your age you should be a *praetor* at least! When did you last give a dinner party?"

Albanus choked on a piece of dry bread. A dinner party! What had this to do with his career?

"With a cook like Bulba?" he queried, raising one eyebrow. "None of my friends would come – or only to mock."

"Actually," said Marilia coyly, 'I wasn't thinking of any of *your* friends particularly. And anyway, let them come, if only to mock. We'll send them away, too surprised to utter a word, except in praise – that's what we'll do! It'll take time, though. I should have taught Metaxus the basics in a month or two."

"My love," Albanus said, "You're going too quickly for me. Are you saying that you are going to teach Metaxus to *cook?* And what about Bulba?"

"Put him out to grass. Literally. Let's see if he can do as much damage to the weeds in the garden as he's been doing to the food in the kitchen."

"Now, I'm not sure that's such a good idea –" Alblanus began, but Marilia interrupted.

"Just leave it to me, my Lord," she said, somehow managing to give this term of wifely respect a mocking edge. Although, the kiss she planted on his florid cheek hinted at other things. He melted.

* * * * *

"So, is married life suiting you?" Marcus inquired, as the warm waters of the tepidarium caressed their limbs.

"For the most part – yes."

"And which part doesn't suit?" asked Marcus, impishly raising one eyebrow.

Albanus sighed. "She's trying to rearrange my life –"

"Nothing bad about that. New broom and everything –"

"She wants to organise a dinner party –"

Marcus threw back his head and bellowed with laughter. "And which of your enemies are you planning on poisoning?"

"She's decided to get rid of Bulba and teach Metaxus to cook instead."

"What, personally? The Greek garden boy? The good-looking one? And you're happy about that, are you?"

"Well, it could be that she's got nothing on her mind but cooking, but... I simply can't imagine what my mother was thinking of, bringing a boy of seventeen into a house with a young bride."

"Can you not?" queried Marcus.

"What are you saying?"

"She was against the marriage, so I understood."

"But she relented –"

"Did she? Did she really? She's not trying to create a little mischief between the two of you, perhaps?

Let's face it: Metaxus could set any woman's pulse racing, slave or no slave."

"But – she's my *mother.*"

"Exactly. We're not just talking about any mother, Albanus. We're talking about Lucopania, *your* mother and, for my part, the mother-in-law from Tartary."

"That bad, eh? She hasn't tried to cause trouble between you and Livilla, surely?"

Marcus threw up his hands and brought them down again with a splash. "You don't know the half of it."

"But – the dinner party –"

"Cancel it."

"Sorry, I don't think I've made myself quite clear. This isn't some bean feast with the neighbours she's planning. It's more like – a banquet."

Marcus whistled through his teeth. "So, who's she talking of inviting?"

"Just a top lawyer or two – and the odd Senator – not to mention the gorgon he calls his wife. One look at Hortensia Mercatrix, so they tell me, and the thought of being turned to stone becomes quite appealing! And it's the past tense: the invitations have gone out already; sent by her, copying my signature and my seal!"

"Albanus, my friend," said Marcus, "you really must bring that wife of yours under control. It's time she learned who wears the toga in your house."

Albanus left the bath house wishing that he could go back to his old, lazy ways of letting life throw whatever detritus at him it liked without his even having to make the effort to avoid it. So deep in his own thoughts was he that he failed to notice a passing litter until the last moment, and the slaves bearing it were forced to judder to a halt as he almost tripped the leader up. The curtain was pulled back abruptly, and a hawk-like nose attached to a long, thin face, poked out. A thatch of bright ginger hair fell no lower than the ears on either side the head, and Albanus was aware of a gleaming white toga. The passenger was not, therefore, a woman, the usual occupant of such a means of conveyance, but a young man – an extremely arrogant young man.

"Do you mind!" he exclaimed, in the high-pitched twang of the aristocrat. "You almost made my men tip me up in the gutter by your foolishness."

"Awfully sorry, old chap," Albanus twanged back. "I'll make sure they manage it next time."

The curtain snapped shut and the litter took off at a trot.

Although Albanus called her name several times on his return from the Baths, Marilia did not come running as usual. He wandered disconsolately through the house, its unaccustomed sparkle and smell of new polish plunging him into further gloom. A murmur of voices and a womanish giggle drew him towards the kitchen. As he pulled back the door curtain, he beheld, facing each other across approximately two feet of floor tiles, Marilia and Metaxus. Had they just sprung apart at his approach? He didn't want to think about it.

"What are you doing?" he inquired wearily.

Marilia at once rushed over to embrace her husband, but he pushed her away. "Not in front of the slaves," he whispered through gritted teeth. He glowered at the ex-gardener, who, forgetting that he was the *ex*-gardener, skulked back to the weeds.

"Don't be angry, my husband," Marilia soothed. "I – well – I was planning a surprise for the dinner party."

"To Hades with the dinner party!" Albanus bellowed, and Marilia at once burst into tears.

Albanus did the only sensible thing in the circumstances: he fled. Once in his study, the room furthest from the unbelievable racket his slip of a wife was making, he sat down at his desk and pressed both hands against his temples. If only he'd heeded the warnings of friends and family. Bringing this girl into his life had been a bad mistake. She had thrown his household and his own emotions into turmoil.

The familiar shuffling of feet and clearing of the throat told him that Galla was in the doorway.

"The Senator Septimus Junius Mercator sends his greetings and awaits you in the atrium, Master," the ancient retainer announced. As Albanus's jaw all but thumped on to his desk, Galla continued in a manner which suggested that Senators were in the habit of calling at the house every other day. "Since he was passing this way, he decided to stop by and accept your dinner invitation in person."

Chapter VII

There were only two classes of Roman male permitted to wear the purple-bordered toga: small boys and senators. It was usually easy enough to tell the difference. The wearer of this exclusive garment, now filling the atrium with his presence, belonged without question to the second category. His height, stately bearing and the silver-grey hair, which descended, full and thick, from the high crown of his head and finished some way above his eyebrows, left Albanus in no doubt that this was the Senator, Septimus Junius Mercator.

Any conversation with his distinguished visitor was out of the question, however, while Marilia's wailing continued to fill every cranny of the house. Albanus's first words were to Galla, therefore.

"Fetch Rebekah, will you. Tell her her mistress needs her."

As the Judaean slave girl, plump as a ripe peach, hurried to calm her mistress, Albanus turned to the Senator, and raised his hands in a gesture of mock despair.

"Woman's troubles," he said, as soon as the noise abated.

"You don't have to explain," the Senator said. "I've had two wives and six daughters. There's nothing I don't know about 'women's troubles!'"

Albanus felt drawn to this man, with his gentle,

yet intelligent eyes. He bitterly regretted that the friendship was doomed before it had had time to breathe the upper air. But before he could tell him the worst, the Senator went on.

"I must congratulate you on your choice of a bride," he said, graciously accepting a cup of wine which Galla had thought it a wise move to produce at that moment. Albanus nearly toppled into the impluvium in surprise. Everyone else of his acquaintance had thought it their duty to warn him off the Gesti family, yet here was a man giving his approval – and that man a Senator no less!

"I regard Titus Marilius Gestus to be an excellent fellow. I believe he deserves to be accepted into Roman society. You know –" He put his free arm around Albanus's shoulder and began pacing him up and down the atrium "– I sometimes think Rome is becoming more provincial than the Provinces. What happened to that noble ideal of welcoming strangers into our midst? Now you, young man, have shown yourself to be a Roman of the old kind – broadminded and open to those who wish to bring their fresh ideas from over the seas."

"I have?" Albanus gulped.

"Indeed. By throwing in your lot with the Gesti and marrying that delightful daughter of theirs, despite her unknown and untried background. I find that a first-rate quality."

"You do?" Albanus struggled not to sound like a complete imbecile. His tongue shot to the roof of his mouth, where it remained stuck as fast as if it had been a stalactite. Otherwise, he might just have blurted out the truth: something like, *Actually, I married her for her money.*

"Now, there's just one thing," the genial old man continued. "I hope I'm not going to upset the seating arrangements."

"The – the seating arrangements? Oh, for the dinner party, you mean?" No sooner had Albanus's tongue worked itself loose than it became stuck again. Otherwise, he might have blurted out something to the effect that, since his wife – that delightful girl – fancies the new slave something rotten, the dinner is therefore cancelled.

"Yes. You see, Hortensia, my dear wife, has unfortunately been summoned to the bedside of her brother. He has a villa near Surrentum. So, I wondered if I could bring instead my protégé – a gifted young man from the provinces. I want to see how he conducts himself at a social occasion."

Despite himself, Albanus felt his head bob up and down like one half of a pair of courting geese. "Ye-es, I can't see there being a problem," said his mouth, entirely of its own volition.

"Excellent!" said the Senator. "Well, I won't keep you. I've obviously dragged you from your study. I look forward to your dinner next week. Very much."

"The dinner party is still on, then?" Marcus raised a quizzical eyebrow.

"Well, what would you have done, with a Senator heaping praise on your head, however undeserved?"

"Difficult, very difficult. Don't get me wrong – I'm not being critical."

"And I expect harmony has been restored at home at least?" This was Livilla's contribution. The trio were seated in the shade provided by the columns of the peristyle surrounding the pleasant garden belonging to Marcus and his wife, Albanus's younger sister: the one who had had the good fortune to take after her father. As they sipped the mellow wine Albanus had come to expect at this house, his three little nieces danced around a sundial, reminding him of The Three Graces.

"On that front," said Albanus, "the answer is, regretfully, no. Marilia still refuses to tell me what she and Metaxus were up to in the kitchen that day. It's a surprise, she says. And I'm wrong not to trust her. Just to prove the point, she has banished me from her bedchamber."

"Poor Albanus," laughed Livilla. "You haven't had an easy start to marriage, have you?"

"Too right – what with that and the dog –"

"The dog?" chorused his sister and brother-in-law.

"Didn't I mention it? We have a dog. I came home early yesterday, to find my house had been turned into some sort of Stygian nightmare." Albanus shuddered at the memory. "I heard screaming even before I'd reached my front door. Once inside, I almost collided with Maia and Thalia, our two house slaves, who were running about like a pair of demented maenads, their tunics hitched up above their knees, while Rebekah clung, shrieking, to Metaxus for protection. The impluvium, meanwhile, had been completely taken over by something that appeared to have escaped from the Underworld: Cerberus, perhaps, or one of his offspring at least. It was huge, yellow, and had paws like paddles, which he was using to splash about with. There was water everywhere, and people sliding about in it, trying to get away."

"Who's Cerberus?" Secunda, Marcus's and Livilla's middle daughter asked, nervously. The trio had joined their parents and uncle on hearing the word 'dog'.

"He's a horrible dog that guards the entrance to Hades," Valeria, her elder sister said, with some relish. "He has three heads and barks fearfully when the dead people try to pass by, and they all tremble and cry lots and lots." She flashed her Uncle Albanus a glorious smile.

At once, Secunda and Tertia, her younger siblings, each buried a face in the tunic of the nearest parent.

"Go on," said Livilla, stroking Tertia's hair. "Where was Marilia in all this?"

"She was cooing and saying daft things like, 'Oh isn't he sweet?' Then, when the creature tried to flatten her with those monstrous paws, and began slobbering all over her face, all she could say was, 'See? He really likes me.'

'Fancies you, anyway,' I answered her, 'for lunch.'"

"Why did she think you needed a dog?" asked Marcus.

"It has everything to do with that silly mosaic Father made to decorate the porch. She couldn't see the point, she said, of having the warning 'Beware of the Dog' if we didn't actually have one, even though this family has managed without one for ever."

"And did you all finally get him under control?" asked Livilla.

"Not before he had dug a hole halfway to Hades in Bulba's prize garden bed, tried to make a meal of my sandals and been stung by a wasp."

"Stung by a wasp?" his audience chorused.

"I'd come home early, as I told you, because I had an appointment at home. Metaxus and Rebekah managed to get the thing into the garden so that Maia and Thalia could clear up the mess in the atrium, before my client came.

"He wasn't the easiest of clients, and Marilia brought us wine and some very good figs from her parents' garden to try softening him up. Next thing, I heard Galla yelling. The beast was rampaging round the garden, destroying everything in sight. Metaxus tried to help me catch him, but when he decided to make a snack of my sandals, I let him have it – struck out with my right hand. However, I was still holding the remains of a very ripe fig, which a passing wasp also fancied. Instead of backing away, like a normal dog would, this animal tried to snap at my hand, and at that moment, the wasp decided to stake his claim, so to speak. He sank his sting into the animal's nose before feasting on the fig."

"Poor creature," Livilla gasped.

"If a dog could scream, he did,' said Albanus. "Metaxus rescued him in the end. He found some vinegar to put on the wound. But now he thinks I was the one who stung him. Every time I come within ten paces of him, he yelps, goes down on his belly and creeps off after Metaxus."

"So, you've decided to keep him, then?"

"Unfortunately, yes. I did try to put Marilia off, by mentioning the expense of feeding an animal that big, but she retaliated by accusing me of thinking about money too much. Says I ought to get out more."

"What's he called?" Secunda asked.

"Your Aunt Marilia wanted to call him *Pulcher.*"

"Beautiful?"

"Yes – which he isn't. I suggested Cerberus, but she said that was being blasphemous."

"I didn't know a dog could be a god," said Livilla.

"Cerberus is immortal, though," said Marcus.

"Anyway, we seem to have compromised on *Rus*, since he has only one head, unlike his namesake, with his three-syllable name to match the number of his heads. Oh, never mind," he added, when he noticed the look that had passed between his sister and brother-in-law.

"He answers to it at least. The trouble is, I no longer know who I am. There's a Senator loose in this city who thinks I'm liberal and broadminded because I've taken a wife with dodgy credentials, and a dog who thinks I have wasp stings in my fingers. What next?"

Albanus dressed for the dinner party with the enthusiasm of a man preparing for his own execution. By contrast, Marilia was as excited as a child anticipating a mountain of presents at the Saturnalia. A cartload of slaves spilled out on to the roadside in the early afternoon, on loan from Titus and Silvia. After they had transformed the atrium and dining-room into miniature hanging gardens, they clustered in the kitchen to receive their orders from Marilia.

At least she had left the choice of wine to Albanus, who, wisely, he thought, had ordered several jars of the best Falernian. If the dinner turned out to be a disaster, he could at least drown himself pleasantly in the finest wine in Rome.

Sweating beneath his crisp, white toga, Albanus waited in the atrium to receive his guests. Galla valiantly sought out the name of each arrival, announcing it to the company in a quavering voice.

"Let me introduce a pupil of mine, lately arrived in Rome from Venusia," the Senator addressed his host. "Leonus Vettius Scaevola." There was only one part of this newcomer which matched his lion-like first name: the thatch of bright ginger hair. For the rest, his body was puny, knee and elbow joints knobbly and the elongated nose and narrow head put Albanus in mind of a bird, most nearly a vulture. The close-set eyes were cold – the same cold pair of eyes he remembered from his near-miss with a certain litter outside the Baths.

Once in the dining-room, the men reclined on the couches which had been arranged on three sides of a large table, while the women were seated, according to custom, on three sides of another, across the room. The fourth sides of each table faced on to the empty space between them, where the promised entertainment would take place.

After the preliminary appetisers, a swan, complete with gold crown, and resting in a lake of violet petals, was carried in, led by two dancing girls. Albanus had to smile. Marilia had been busy indeed. Here were Maia and Thalia, dressed as naiads. The bird, once dismantled and served on silver plates, turned out to be mullet, excellently cooked in red wine.

Albanus barely heard the compliments being heaped on his and his wife's heads as each dish was savoured and devoured. He was conscious only of the young puppy, Leonus, who was having great difficulty in controlling his paws. He seemed to find it necessary to run a hand up and down the torso of whatever slave was attending to him. It was only a matter of time, give or take a few more goblets of wine, before he would start on the guests. With every mouthful of that expensive beverage, his tongue grew wilder, his jokes more offensive and his voice drowned out all the other guests' attempts at conversation.

As the dishes were being cleared away, there came a commotion from the kitchen, at which Marilia excused herself. Before she could return, the main entertainment of the evening began.

A single pipe began to play, the notes rhythmic and exotic. From behind the door curtain, a figure slowly emerged. Eyes, rendered huge by the use of aquamarine paint, dwarfed the small face. A black wig, plaited, Egyptian fashion, into tiny, straight braids, covered the dancer's own hair. Her gently swaying hips made elegant and seductive sweeps of her long, white, pleated tunic. Arms, encased in wide gold bangles, rose in the air, weaving around each other, snake-like, to the rhythm of the pipe. Enchantment filled the room. All became lost in the magic of the dance. At its climax, the dancer approached the table, removed the gilded bandeau from around her own hair and placed it on the Senator's distinguished grey head.

All through the dance, Albanus had been only too aware of the empty space where Marilia should have been sitting. For him, there was no mystery as to who the dancer was: only how she could have got her make-up on so quickly. Then, as the dancer began to sway out of the dining-room, all of Tartary broke loose.

Leonus thrust out an arm and grasped the dancer's skirt, tugging her backwards, before wrapping both arms around her waist and lifting her off her feet. The dancer, her writhing body partly on the couch and partly on Leonus, retaliated with a swift blow aimed at his head, which he dodged with practised skill. He grabbed for the offending hand, but instead she brought his up to her scarlet mouth, sinking her teeth into it with all the ferocity of a mad dog. Meanwhile her wig had skewed round, so that half the braids hung over her face, covering her nose and one eye.

"By all the gods!" Albanus exclaimed. The dancer's own hair, now revealed on one side of her head, was short, curly and tinted with copper.

"Metaxus!" he breathed. A scene flashed before his eyes: his young wife and the gardener-turned-cook in the kitchen, facing each other companionably. So that was what they were up to the day he had returned from the Baths. Marilia had been teaching Metaxus to dance!

At this moment, the figure of Marilia filled the doorway. With imperious calm, she took charge. At the snap of her fingers, two slaves came running, prising the enraged cook off the Senator's young apprentice. Bowls of warm water and towels were brought and the bleeding wound attended to. Albanus felt obliged to apologise to the Senator for this outrage to a guest, although the words all but choked him.

Septimus's response was to ask for a litter to be brought to take Leonus home.

"It is I who owe you an apology," the old man said. "I wanted to give that young puppy the benefit of the doubt. Unfortunately, my worst fears have come true. He's no more than a provincial thug. I'll have him conveyed to his own bed, so that we can enjoy the rest of the evening in peace."

Wine is a great leavener, and, with the god

Bacchus on Albanus's side, the party was soon swinging along good-humouredly once more. The guests departed at about dawn, and then only reluctantly. The Senator was the last to leave.

"I must thank you and your charming wife for your hospitality. After tonight, I fear there will be a vacancy for a student at law in my household. You wouldn't be interested, perhaps? Could you call on me tomorrow? Late afternoon would be best."

His head spinning, though not only from the wine, Albanus set about finding Marilia. If she was still awake, he wanted to share his good news with her. A sound reached his ears, low and muffled, like the sound of weeping. As he approached Marilia's bed-chamber, it grew louder. In her long, white tunic, arranged like a bridal dress, she lay, resting her head against her embroidered pillow, and quietly sobbing.

"My love!" he exclaimed, entering the room and placing his arms about her soft, warm body. "What has upset you? You should be happy. The dinner party was a masterpiece."

"It was a fiasco!" sobbed his wife. "Metaxus bit a *guest*. That means he'll have to be crucified at least!" She threw her head back and wailed.

"Well, actually," Albanus began, "I was thinking of rewarding him."

"*Rewarding* him?"

"Yes – by giving him his freedom. If he hadn't bit that young upstart, I might have done it myself. He hadn't got a clue about the laws of hospitality: fingering up my staff and shouting like a market trader all through dinner."

"I don't suppose his sort thinks of slaves as anything more than objects," said Marilia.

"Which is one more black mark against him," Albanus retorted. "They are members of my household, and no one touches them without my permission."

Marilia gazed adoringly at her husband. "You're such a good man, Albanus. And giving Metaxus his freedom is a very thoughtful thing to do, but, I wonder, do you think you could put it off for a few years?"

"If you like, but why? How many years were you thinking of?"

"Say, about ten? It's just that I've got more plans for him. Did you know that he knows the Homeric Epics by heart?"

"It wouldn't surprise me in the least," said Albanus, flatly. "Is there any limit to his talents?"

"None," said his wife, oblivious to his sarcasm. She had quite forgotten her tears. "He's a real find – we must thank your mother properly. Now, I was thinking of having him double as a tutor for our little one."

"But we don't have a little one –" Albanus's voice tailed off as he stared into the laughing eyes of his young wife. "You mean – you? Me? Us?"

Marilia's laughter rang through the house. "That's what I love about you," she said at last, rising on to her knees and kissing the top of his head, where his receding hairline began. "You're so quick on the uptake."

The next day, having spent even longer at the Baths than he had on his wedding-day, Albanus set out for the home of Septimus Mercator on the Palatine Hill. The day was exceptional in every way. A cool breeze lightened his way. Birds sang in the trees; his heart sang with the knowledge that his beautiful wife loved him and that he was to become a father.

As he began the final steep climb up the leafy avenue towards the Senator's house, he was only vaguely aware of the sound of cartwheels. Seconds later, hands grasped him round the throat and pulled him backwards. Heavy, rough material enveloped him as the stink of rotten vegetation filled his nostrils and his lungs gasped for air. Arms lifted him off the ground; one minute, he was being bundled over something upright, like the side of a cart; the next he had landed heavily on a lumpy surface. Cartwheels rumbled under him, their movement throwing him hard against the wooden plank at the far end.

Chapter VIII

Albanus struggled for air inside the rough bag. The vile smell flooded his nostrils and made him retch, while dust caught in his throat, so that every breath was an agonising wheeze. The speeding cart bumped over the cobbles and bounced him from side to side. Just as darkness – not just the semi-dark of the inside of the bag, but a painful darkness inside his own head, preceded by a spinning galaxy of stars – was about to overtake him, the cart lurched to a halt, and he was pulled and dragged until he thumped on to sharp stones on the ground, then pulled some more across a rough surface. Finally, as the sack was tugged off his head, a nasal voice screamed in his ear.

"Stay right where you are!" it screeched. "Don't move!"

Albanus, despite the bruises and pain in his lungs, managed to mutter, "No, Jupiter, please not Leonus Scaevola –"

But when he opened his eyes, he beheld the vulturine features which he had already seen enough of to last him a lifetime. The face wore a frown so deep that the already too close eyes seemed almost to overlap.

"Got to stop meeting like this, old chap –" Albanus began.

"Shut up!" shrilled the other. "I want to talk to you. You had better listen."

"Actually," said Albanus, sweeping a potato peeling off the side of his mouth, "I'd rather eat pigswill."

The eyes overlapped still further. "Thanks to you, I've lost my position with Septimus Mercator."

"Nothing to do with me. You managed that pretty well on your own. But I don't suppose you remember much about it –"

"Silence!!" screamed the young man. "Not only that, you're about to usurp my place. Well, that's not going to happen. Understand?" He grabbed at Albanus's now filthy toga, and glared into his face. "You have a very pretty wife."

Albanus took in a sharp breath. "No! Please!"

"Just keep away from the Senator, or I'll make sure she doesn't stay that way. And as for your father-in-law, don't make me let the authorities know exactly who he is. Believe me, it's not pretty, either."

Leonus let go and pushed Albanus to the ground. Then he and his companions, who had all this time been lurking in the shadows, swaggered outside and soon Albanus heard the rumbling of cartwheels once more. Albanus looked about him: he was in some kind of barn, he guessed; the remnants of a farm before the City overran this part of the countryside. He looked down at the wreck he had become. Rotten tomatoes, slime from an overripe marrow and the remnants of someone's cooking, and not that recent – probably intended as a delicacy for pigs – covered him from the top of his bald head to his sandals. He reeked with the odour of all things rotten. As he rolled over and tried to rise, he winced and groaned. Every movement hurt. Breathing heavily, like a man twice his age, he heaved himself upright and began limping towards the sunlight in the yard across which he had been dragged in the sack.

Three hours later, he finally struggled up the Caelian Hill and banged on his own front door. Galla was well used to the various states of inebriation and intoxication in which his master frequently fell through the door, but the sight of him this time left him totally speechless. It was Marilia who rushed to his side, held him gently but at arms' length and guided him straight out into the peristyle, before calling out all the young members of the household to sluice her husband down.

Thalia, Maia, Rebekah and Metaxus duly paraded out into the sunshine, each bearing a jug or bucket, whose contents they promptly emptied over the head of their hapless master. This gave rise to such hilarity that Albanus began plotting a mass crucifixion of all his slaves. Once their vessels were empty, they ran to the fountain for a re-fill with which to dowse him and each other. Soon a major water-fight was in progress. Rus joyfully joined in, barking ecstatically and sinking his teeth into anything that moved.

Shivering and soaked through, Albanus finally dragged himself to his feet and struggled back into the house, leaving the young slaves to their game. Scolding him for leaving a trail of water on the marble floor, Marilia nevertheless gently towelled him down and tucked him into his bed with a steaming cup of something that smelled deliciously of honey and herbs.

When she had heard most of the story, she called Metaxus. "Go to the home of the Senator now," she ordered him. "He must know what has happened."

"No," Albanus protested. "Just tell him I have been taken ill. Do not tell him anything else."

Metaxus, whose comprehension of Latin had greatly improved, though he spoke it less well, nodded politely. "I take Rus?" he enquired.

"He'll run wild," said Albanus.

"I have –" He made a gesture indicating something snake-like.

"Rebekah has woven a lead for Rus," Marilia explained.

"Rebekah! Well, well," said Albanus.

With Metaxus and Rus gone, Marilia turned to her husband. "Why don't you want Septimus to know about the kidnap?' she asked. "Surely he needs to be informed as soon as possible."

"I didn't tell you everything Leonus said," Albanus replied, drawing her on to the bed. "He threatened to expose your father. Said something about telling the whole Senate who he really is, and that it wasn't 'pretty'. That's the word he used, 'pretty'."

Marilia sat still a long time. At last, she said, "I know that there's a reason why Father left Rome –"

"*Left* Rome? I understood that he had only lately come to Rome, that he came originally from Spain –"

"He moved to Rome from somewhere north of

here, once he had started his merchant's business. He and Mama had to leave in a hurry but I never found out why."

Albanus whistled through his teeth. "I need to find out," he said at last.

"How would this – Leonus, did you say? – know about Father? You never introduced him to me at the Dinner party. I was in and out, as you know, seeing to the arrangements. What are his other names?"

Albanus scratched his head. "Er – Vet-something."

"And his surname?" There was an urgency in her tone.

"Scavenus – something like that."

"Or Scaevola?" Marilia had leaped off the bed and was clinging on to a door curtain for support. "Vettius Scaevola? From Venusia?"

"That's it. But how did…" His voice tailed away, as his young wife sank to the floor.

"Oh, Jupiter," she murmured. "Oh, Jupiter Almighty."

"What?" Albanus cried, rising as fast as the bruises to his arms and legs would allow.

"He's a relation of ours," Marilia wailed. "We are undone!"

Now, it was Albanus's turn to support his wife. Ignoring his own aching joints, he lifted her up gently and led her to the bed.

"Try not to get too upset," he said, placing pillows behind her head, then sitting beside her.

"Remember the baby –"

"I can't help being upset," Marilia sobbed. "When we were planning to come back here, papa changed his name from Titus Vettius Rufus to Titus Marilius Gestus. We are Vetii, also!"

"Leonus is probably only a distant relative," Albanus tried to comfort his wife.

"No, he isn't. Papa had an uncle, also called Leonus Vettius Scaevola. A class one scoundrel, he called him."

Not the only one, thought Albanus.

"This could be his grandson. But how could he have guessed who we are? I must warn Papa." Marilia began to rise from the bed.

"It's very late," Albanus said, gently pushing her back on to the pillows. "Neither of us is quite the picture of health right now. Tomorrow will have to do."

Marilia protested only briefly. Soon, she had fallen asleep. Sleep did not come as easily to Albanus. Whichever way he lay, a joint or a muscle protested. His head ached and his mind was in a spin.

The next morning, Albanus summoned Metaxus. Although it pained him to ask, he needed to know Septimus's reaction to his failure to keep the appointment.

Metaxus searched the ceiling for the right words. "Hee's lady send me to Reever," the young cook said at last. "He walking by Teeber. He give me thanks, then I go here." He pointed at the floor.

"Thank you for that," said Albanus. "Now, I'd

like you to take another message to the Forum. I will give you directions. I am still not well, so I shall not be at the Law Courts today." He handed Metaxus a note. "You may take the rest of the day off. We shall not need lunch, only a small supper." The young Greek smiled and left.

Albanus and Marilia allowed themselves the luxury of a litter to convey them to the home of Titus and Silvia. Titus was still busy with his morning's clients when they alighted outside the impressive door to the house, but Silvia and little Sextus greeted them delightedly.

While they were enjoying a cup of wine, Titus appeared, and seemed equally pleased at their visit. Albanus prayed to whatever god happened to be listening at that moment that Titus's reason for fleeing Rome was not so serious that he would be forced to dislike his father-in-law. At this moment, he liked him more than anyone he knew, besides his wife and Marcus. He was feeling more and more comfortable in the presence of his in-laws.

At last, Marilia moved to the edge of her chair, and began, "Pater... we have some news. Not very good news."

She then blurted out the story of Albanus's encounter with Leonus and his threat. Silvia clung to her husband's arm throughout this speech, her eyes as large as sunflowers, fixed and staring. Titus, on the other hand, looked perfectly relaxed.

"Well, you're right about Leonus. He's your

second cousin. It sounds as though he's a chip off the old block all right."

"We need to get him out of Rome, Papa," said Marilia.

"That would be a good idea in the circumstances – just until I can seek an audience with the Emperor."

"With the Emperor?" echoed everyone else in the room, except Silvia.

"Sire," Albanus began. "You may not want to trust me on this, but could you tell me – and Marilia, of course – just what made you flee Rome in the first place?"

Titus fixed his bright, shrewd eyes on his son-in-law.

"I trusted you when I chose to introduce you to my daughter as a possible marriage partner," he said, "and I trust you still. What would you say that my dear wife, here, and I fled Rome to avoid being accused of attempted murder?"

Only Silvia's quiet sobbing broke the silence that followed Titus's words. Even the marble busts on their stands around the room seemed to be holding their breath. At last, Marilia, who was comforting her mother, said, "Tell us, Papa."

"When I came to Rome, in the third year of the reign of the Divine Domitian," Titus began, "I seemed to have the Midas touch. My business took off at an extraordinary rate. I was in demand for everything from the best spices to the most desirable works of art. I took orders from the ordinary populace, patricians and members of the Royal household alike. As you know, Domitian, one of our greatest Emperors, had no children to succeed him. What hardly anyone knows is that he had adopted a young relative, one Lucius, of whom he was very fond, and whom he was grooming to be his successor. Alas, in this one respect, he showed a terrible lack of judgement. Rome would have been destroyed by him had he become Emperor. Among his more unsocial habits was his way of disposing of his servants at intervals, to avoid any of his more intimate secrets from leaking out. He used to have his physicians beheaded for the same reason.

"Then, one day, I was summoned to the palace. I thought that Domitian wanted to see me, so imagine my discomfort when I was taken to the quarters of Lucius. When we were alone, he showed me where he was losing his hair. He was one of those handsome youths – far too good-looking for his own good – and his appearance was everything. Vanity in leather sandals. He wanted me to acquire a wig from the best source available. I had been importing wigs from the East for some time, and expressed my willingness to oblige. At the same time, I was quaking in my boots. I knew that my days in Rome were numbered. I returned home and warned Silvia that we would have to start packing almost immediately. Why we didn't leave within the week, I still don't know. Instead, I ordered the wig and, when it arrived two months later, took it to Lucius.

"He was delighted, and paid me handsomely.

But, praise the gods, we were poised for flight. The next day, one of Lucius's bodyguards passed by with a warning. Lucius had been taken ill in the night, and was planning to have me arrested, for poisoning the wig. What quarrel did I have with him? I wanted to know. The bodyguard replied that it didn't work that way, and I should leave as soon as possible. Silvia and I fled the same night."

Another silence. Even Silvia had dried her eyes.

"What became of Lucius?" Albanus asked.

"He died a few years later, of poisoning. No one was blamed. The case remains open to this day."

"And what brought you back to Rome?"

"Domitian was dead; so was Nerva, who succeeded him. I felt that Trajan would feel disposed to grant me a pardon."

"But to come back to Rome before the pardon was granted – wasn't that a bit risky?"

"I'd hoped to obtain a pardon while we were still in Egypt, but, as you know, Trajan has been busy these last ten years on his military campaigns. He was too busy to look into the case of one small merchant. Then Marilia was growing up. She had passed the age when most Roman girls marry, and I was determined that she should have a Roman husband – that we could all live peacefully in the new Rome created by Trajan. So, I took the clan name of Marilius, from the region of Spain where we first lived, adopted the surname of Gestus from my mother's side of the family, and here you see us."

"You're extremely — brave," said Albanus, struggling to find the right adjective.

"'Foolhardy' is the word you were looking for, I think," said Titus, without smiling. "I have put all my family at risk."

"You did the only thing you could, Papa," said Marilia. They exchanged a look which was loaded with meaning. Albanus thought better of asking just what it did mean. Instead, he thanked his father-in-law for being so open.

As they had half expected, Silvia insisted that they stayed for lunch, and after consuming freshly baked bread dipped in olive oil, a quantity of nuts and home-grown figs, they were back at their own house by early evening.

"I still think we must get rid of Leonus somehow," said Marilia, as they strolled up the Caelian Hill. "That'll give Papa time to make his deputation to the Emperor."

"What your father doesn't realise is that by being in Rome he is probably committing an illegal act," said Albanus. "He should have been making a plea while still in exile."

"But he was never banished. He chose to leave."

"We need someone of influence to speak up for him — someone like Septimus Mercator. But I'm wary of approaching him. What if Leonus's spies find out? Your father could be banished a second time — or tried and found guilty for returning to Rome illegally."

He omitted Leonus's other veiled threat, the one

concerning Marilia herself, but this, naturally, troubled him more.

As they reached the house, Albanus was aware of a snuffling sound and something nudging the back of his knee. He turned round and was immediately pinned against the door by a pair of paddles on the end of two furry legs. A tongue, which could have stretched from there to Hades, proceeded to cover his face with spittle.

"Rus! Get off me!"

"Excuse, Master." Metaxus, laden with a basket of produce from the market, struggled to restrain the hound.

"I didn't know you were behind us," said Marilia, wondering what the cook had overheard. Metaxus resorted to a trick he had learned, when he chose not to understand what was being said to him, and gave her a blank, innocent stare.

Not long afterwards, when he had unloaded his shopping, the young Greek was again seen heading to the door, Rus in front and tugging him eagerly.

"Where are you going this time?" Marilia asked.

"Back to market. I forget item."

"What exactly?"

"Just – item."

"But it's late."

"Maybe I catch market before close," called the slave over his shoulder, as Rus dragged him out into the street.

"I fear our cook has taken himself off on an errand," Marilia said to her husband. "Which probably means that we shall have to forage for ourselves if we want any supper."

"That would suit me fine," said Albanus. "I'm aching all over. Let's have a few olives in the peristyle, and a glass of wine, followed by an early night."

Thus they sat companionably in the cool of the evening, a bowl of nuts and olives between them, listening to the fountain playing its merry tune. The pains in his limbs and back eased with each sip he took and Albanus breathed in the sweet smell of the triangles of lawn with a growing sense of peace.

It was time, thought Albanus, that another little matter was cleared up.

"My dear," he began, "I couldn't help noticing the look that passed between you and your father this evening, when you said something about not having any choice about returning to Rome. Not another little bit of trouble in the provinces, was there?"

Marilia looked puzzled for a moment, then laughed briefly. "No, it was nothing like that. I was the cause, actually."

"You?"

"Yes." She let out a sigh. "There was — someone, in Egypt. We were in love, if you want to know. I met him in the market. We kept our meetings secret, at first, because his family were Judaean. He worshipped the One True God, as he put it, and if we'd have married he'd have had to give up his family and his faith. It was too much to ask.

"When my father found out, he promised me

that he would find me a good husband in Rome. There wasn't much chance that I'd find one myself, not with us being unknown in the City. I trusted him, and here –" she drew close to Albanus and laid her head on his shoulder "– he hasn't disappointed me. He's an excellent judge of character, you know. And so is the Senator, it seems. You're a good man, Albanus, a wonderful man."

A commotion somewhere in the house, accompanied by the sound of excited barking, roused them both.

"What now?" said Albanus, wearily, regretting that the magic of the moment was being interrupted.

"Master!" Galla, moving faster than he had done in years, was wheezing in the doorway behind them. "Metaxus has pulled the Senator out of the Tiber!"

He could have been Neptune himself, dripping on to the marble floor of the atrium, if it had not been for the fact that he was bent over and wheezing. His soggy toga, once a sparkling white, but now stained grey-green, dragged behind him, and various strands of slimy vegetation streamed down his beard. Rus, though in better spirits, was also trailing river water and green slime. As Albanus drew closer to his unexpected guest, the dog wagged his tail in greeting, then shook his shaggy coat so that stinking droplets flew in all directions.

There was no sluicing down with freezing fountain water for the Senator, however, unlike the treatment meted out to Albanus by his beloved the day before. Septimus Junius might not have been drowned in pigswill, as Albanus had, but Tiber water gave off just as evil a smell. Marilia clapped her hands and rallied the slaves, Maia and Thalia, to prepare a bathtub with hot water, Rebekah to bring hot towels. Albanus was dispatched to find a clean tunic and toga, Bulba to see to Rus, and Metaxus to prepare a warming stew. She, herself, mixed a curious cocktail of warm wine, honey and herbs.

Once Galla had attended the Senator in his bathing and dressing, the refreshing aroma of eucalyptus oil came seeping through the house.

Restored to the dignity with which the household had come to associate him, the Senator at last felt able to join his hosts, who were awaiting him in the peristyle. Here, Metaxus presented him with a bowl of lamb stew and Marilia persuaded him to try her drink.

"This will soothe the nerves and restore vigour," she assured him. "And prevent any illness resulting from swallowing Tiber water," she added more softly.

"You're kindness itself, my dear," Septimus Junius murmured, briefly touching Marilia's hand. He still saw her as a child, rather than a young bride, thought Albanus, without annoyance or jealousy.

"Tell me, sire," Albanus began, "What could have caused you to fall into the river?"

"Oh, I didn't fall." Septimus turned a bright eye towards his host. "I was pushed."

Marilia gasped. "Are you sure?"

"I always take a walk along the bank of the river about this time," said Septimus. "In the cool of the day, when a feeling of calm lies over the city. It's very quiet just there. Your man, Metaxus, found me there last evening, if I remember, to pass on the message that you had met with some misfortune."

"I – yes, I remember. I must give you my apologies again. I deeply regret that I was unable to avail myself of your most generous offer –" Here, Albanus broke off. He could feel his face glowing with a warmth which had nothing to do with the temperature in the peristyle. There was still too much unfinished business with one knobbly-kneed, carrot-headed young waste-of-space before he could hope for any favours from the Senator.

But Septimus reached out and touched his arm. "Speak to me another day of that," he said, gently. "Word did reach me of your unfortunate accident."

"So, it was Metaxus who just happened to find you in the water – when you were pushed, that is?"

Marilia brought the men round to the most recent event. "Did he say whether he'd seen anything?"

"Best ask him," the Senator replied.

Summoned from the kitchen, Metaxus stood calmly before his inquisitors. Albanus wondered if the others were aware of the quiet dignity of the young slave, who had never taken his position very seriously.

"We want to ask you a question, Metaxus," said Albanus. "Did you see Senator Septimus Junius fall into the Tiber River?"

"Yes, Master."

"How did it happen?'

'He get –" Metaxus hunted for the right word, failed, and reached out both hands, palms forward, in a pushing motion.

"Did you see who did this?"

"Man in toga," came the confident reply.

"Well," said Albanus, "that narrows it down to about twenty thousand. Did you recognise this man?"

Metaxus indicated someone rather deficient in terms of height. "But I don't see head."

"He was headless?" exclaimed Marilia, and Rebekah, standing in the doorway, shrieked.

"He cover head with toga," came the reply. "He have big toga, and he little man. He put it over head."

"What were you doing on that part of the bank?" Marilia sounded suspicious.

"I see man, Domina," Metaxus answered, with a bow towards his mistress. "He try to hide, behind tree, bush, stone, anything. So I follow. Then I see Senator. I see man following Senator. Then, when Senator stand in front of river, he run, very quietly, and –" again the pushing motion with the hands and arms.

"I see," said Albanus. "Were there no other witnesses? Did you not see anyone else on the bank?"

"I see no one."

At this point, Septimus spoke. "He's right. There was no one else there. I was just so fortunate that this young man was abroad with your dog. I was being dragged under by the weight of my clothing, and the Tiber, as you know, is a very fast-flowing river. Praise the gods, the dog is a big, strong brute. He pulled me out."

"And, apart from the fact that he was short" – Albanus was addressing Metaxus – "you weren't able to pick out anything else about this man who, you say, pushed the Senator in?"

A slightly mischievous gleam entered the young slave's eye. "He have –" He placed a hooked finger in front of his face, "– big nose. And eyes –" Here, he lifted up two fingers, then crossed them.

"Scaevola." Three voices spoke the name at once. "Leonus Vettius Scaevola."

"Now that I think of it," the Senator put in, "I had had a bit of an altercation with him earlier, but I thought we had settled the matter. He's not taken too kindly to being dismissed from my tutelage, you understand."

"How much earlier?" Albanus asked.

"Oh, only about half an hour or so. Such a pity we can't use this young man's evidence in a court of law," murmured Septimus, shaking his head.

"We could…" said Albanus.

"Except that your young man is a slave, and, as you know, slaves' evidence is only accepted under torture. I couldn't do such a thing to someone who has just saved my life. And I did so want to get rid of that young monkey. He's probably been responsible for more murders in the past three months than the rest of the Roman underworld put together."

"We don't have to have him brought to trial, though," said Marilia. "Just spread it about in all the drinking houses that his number is up, and he'll probably go into voluntary exile."

"*We* should be so lucky," muttered Albanus. "No, we'll have to use Metaxus's evidence."

"But – they'll torture him," Marilia cried, "just as the Senator said!"

"Oh, did I forget to tell you?" said Albanus. "I gave Metaxus his freedom this morning."

Marilia screamed and flung her arms about her husband's neck.

"Not now, my dear," Albanus whispered in his

wife's ear, at the same time gently untangling her soft limbs. To the Senator, he said, "I must apologise for my wife's behaviour, sire."

"Not at all," the old man responded. "Very appropriate in the circumstances. Well then," he continued, smiling, "on the boy's evidence, Scaevola is as good as banished. Oh, did I say that the job's still yours if you want it, young man?" He turned to Albanus, who spluttered into his tunic in confusion.

"Senator…" Marilia began, "there's a favour I need to ask you."

"Any favour I can bestow – it's yours," said the old man graciously. He sat listening to her father's story while the sky darkened and the cicadas in the shrubs began their night music.

When she came to the end, he said solemnly, "I'll have a word with the Emperor at the first opportunity. I should be delighted to help your father to gain a pardon."

After the Senator had finally departed, Marilia again threw her arms about her husband's neck.

"You're a great man, a really good man. My father chose well for me."

"Goodness, what's brought this on?" asked a delighted Albanus.

"Giving Metaxus his freedom like that, of course."

"You don't really believe all that nonsense about seeing Scaevola push the Senator into the river do you?"

"Why? Don't you?"

"Of course not. Far too much of a coincidence."

"So, who did? You don't mean…?"

"That scallywag, Metaxus. He did it himself."

"But why?"

"Why? Where do I begin? Appearing to save the Senator's life, to get him here where we could finish the job by dancing attendance on him, so that he felt obliged to offer me the job once more, and help get a pardon for your dad, incriminating Leonus into the bargain. Need I go on?"

Marilia pursed her lips. "But Metaxus' evidence will be a lie."

"Is that a problem? Scaevola is guilty of so many crimes for which he hasn't been convicted, what does it matter if he's convicted of something he didn't do?"

"You know Metaxus and Rebekah have been in love since, well, for ever?"

"No," said Albanus, surprised.

"Well, they have. So… do you think you might just consider giving her her freedom as well, so that they can marry? As a sort of wedding gift?"

"A wedding gift for a wedding gift? I like it." Albanus gave his wife a hug.

* * * * * * * * * * * * *

Six months later, a party was gathered in the peristyle, where scented wax candles perfumed and illuminated the garden. The guests included Livilla, Marcus and their little girls, Lucopania, Cordelia and her brood, not to mention Titus, Silvia and Sextus. The Senator and his wife were the guests of honour, so that Titus could thank them in person for their influence in obtaining a pardon from the Emperor. Titus could now revert to his former name of Titus Vettius Rufus, although Marilia had strong views on being re-named Vettia.

"If anyone calls me that, I simply won't answer," she announced. She then let out a cry of pain, crumpled and clutched her abdomen.

Lucopania was on her feet in an instant. "Inside with you, my girl," she commanded. "Midwifery is one of my many talents. Didn't that husband of yours tell you that? Rally the slaves! All hands to their posts!"

While the male guests remained outside, trying to keep some sort of conversation going, the women hurried into the house. Some hours, and several jugs of wine later, Lucopania came out bearing a tiny bundle.

"Marilia has been delivered of a healthy girl," she announced, carefully placing the bundle on the stone floor, as was the custom. "Albanus, please pick your daughter up if you wish to acknowledge her as your own. And do take care to support her head."

Nervously, Albanus bent down and, having decided which end *was* her head, picked the infant up.

"Name?" Lucopania prompted him.

"Er – Cordelia, of course. Cordelia Marililla." His words were greeted by cheers and the raising of goblets all around him.

Cradling his daughter, Albanus stumbled across

to his wife's bedroom, returning about an hour afterwards, empty-handed.

"Is my daughter well?" Titus inquired of his son-in-law.

"I should say so," Albanus replied. "She's only planning the next dinner party!"

The End

About the Author

Monica Withrington was born and educated in South Africa. Although trained as a teacher, she has told and written stories all her life, some of which have been published. She now lives in the Midlands, where she enjoys the inspiration she receives from her four granddaughters. Her many books can all be found on Amazon.